MILLIONS OF YEARS AGO

prehistoric *TRUCKS* roamed the earth.

They were *HUGE.*

They were *HUNGRY.*

But they weren't helpful like they are today.

They rumbled, roared, and chomped.

And they did *NOT* get along well with others.

They were called . . .

Little, Brown and Company • Hachette Book Group
237 Park Avenue, New York, NY 10017
Visit our website at www.lb-kids.com

Little, Brown and Company is a division of
Hachette Book Group, Inc.
The Little, Brown name and logo are trademarks of
Hachette Book Group, Inc.

First Paperback Edition: May 2012
First published in hardcover in 2009 by Little, Brown and Company
Library of Congress Cataloging-in-Publication Data
Gall, Chris.
Dinotrux / written and illustrated by Chris Gall.—1st ed.
p. cm.
Summary: Millions of years ago, the prehistoric ancestors of today's
trucks, such as Garbageadon, Dozeratops, and Craneosaurus, roamed the
Earth until they rusted out and became extinct.
ISBN 978-0-316-02777-9 (hc) / 978-0-316-13392-0 (pb)
[1. Imaginary creatures—Fiction. 2. Trucks—Fiction.] I. Title.
PZ7.G1352Tr 2009
[E]—dc22
2008027531

10 9 8 7 6 5 4 3 2 1
SC • Printed in China

The text was set in Cafeteria Black, and the display type
is hand-lettered. The artwork for this book was created
using bearskins and stone knives.

Ⓛ Ⓑ

LITTLE, BROWN AND COMPANY
New York Boston

The earth was **FIERY** and **DANGEROUS.**
Volcanoes shot lava everywhere.
Cave people ran for their lives—
and tar pits could swallow them whole.

LOOK! High in the branches . . .
CRANEOSAURUS!

He was always sticking his nose
where it didn't belong.

CRACK, MUNCH.

Look out, birds, it's time for lunch!

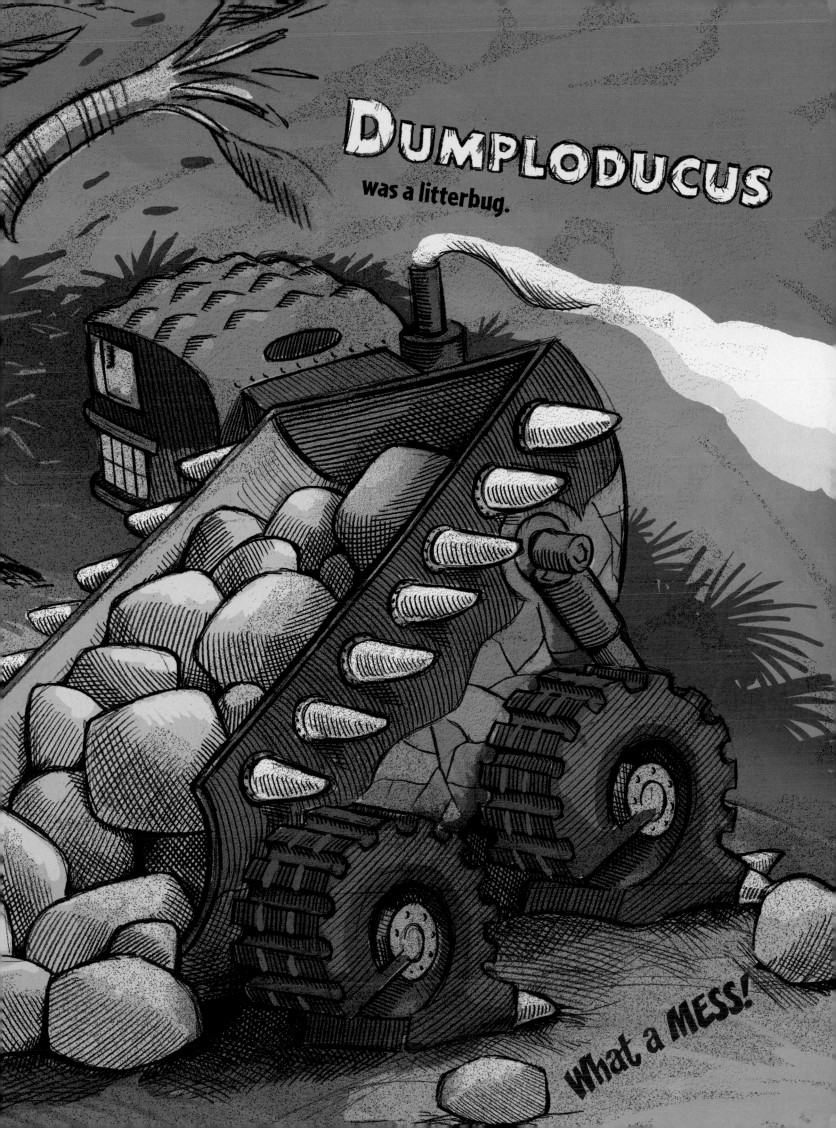

That rascal **DIGASAURUS** used his shovel wherever he pleased.

Mmmmm, dirt!

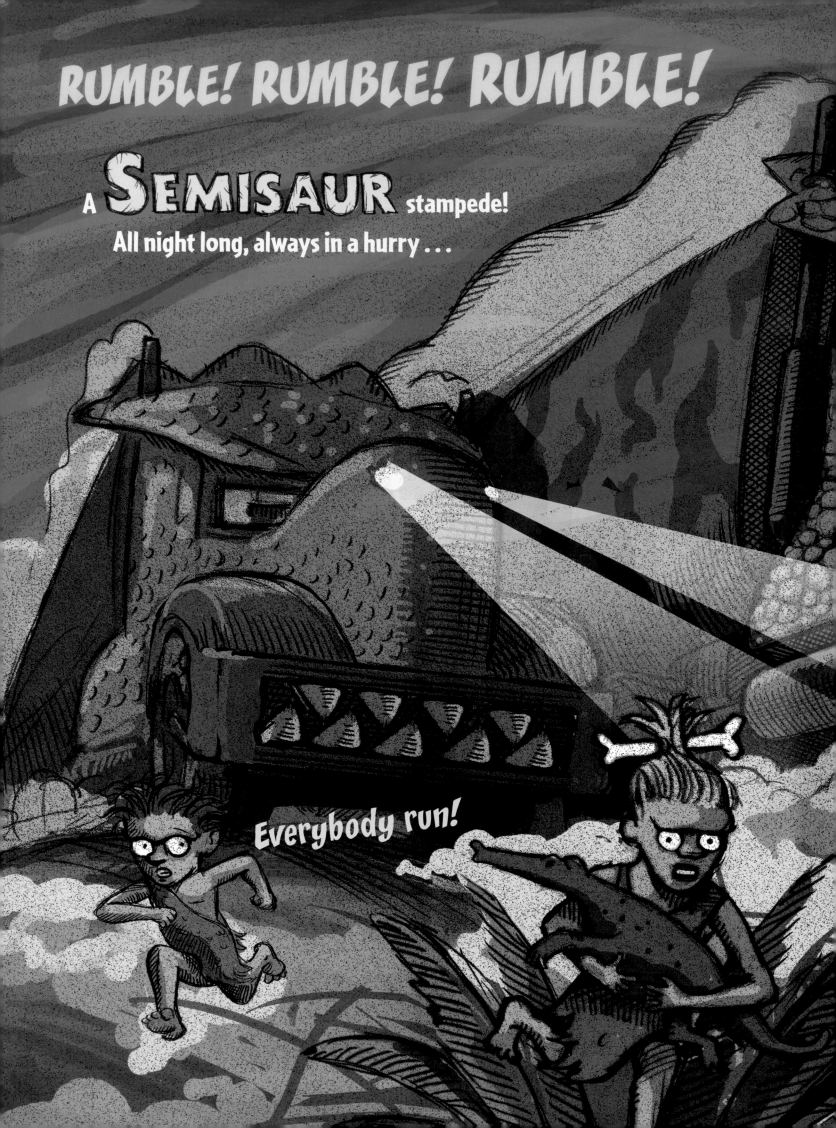

BOOM! BOOM! BOOM!

Look out! It's the bully of the jungle!

Get away, TANKERSAURUS –

Don't spill on his foot!

CHOMPING, ROLLING, DIGGING,

HONKING . . .

the Dinotrux ruled for a million years or more.
But one day, there was a flash of light and a terrible storm.

Dinotrux everywhere **WHEEZED** and **SNEEZED.**

Most began to rust.

They slowly sank into the goo and mud.

But the smart ones went south in search of better weather.
And over the **HUNDREDS**
and **THOUSANDS**
and **MILLIONS** of years,

Good work, Dinotrux!
Now they're **ALWAYS** on the job . . .

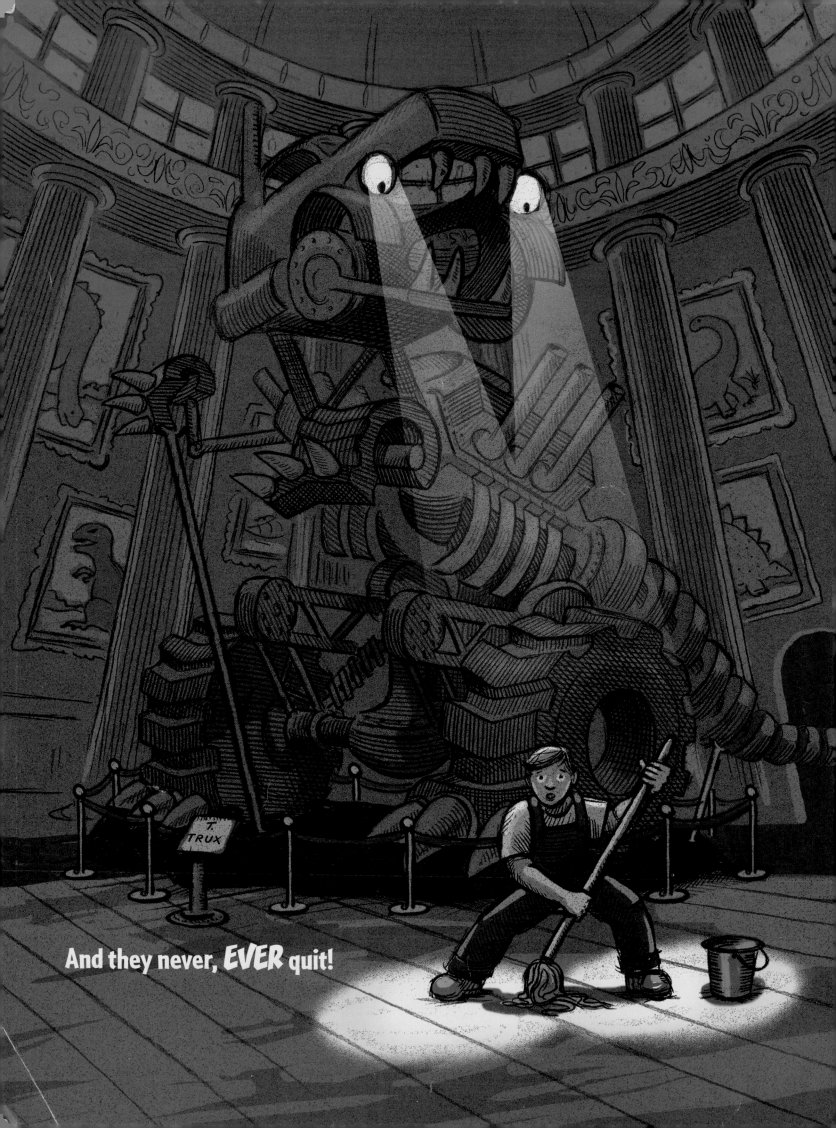

And they never, **EVER** quit!